TREASURE HUNT

By Maria S. Barbo
Illustrated by Duendes del Sur
Hello Reader — Level 1

ISBN 0-439-31849-1

20 19 18 17 16 15 14 13   08 09 10 11 12 13/0

Designed by Maria Stasavage
Printed in the U.S.A.
First Scholastic printing, April 2002

SCHOLASTIC INC.
New York   Toronto   London   Auckland   Sydney
Mexico City   New Delhi   Hong Kong   Buenos Aires

and his friends were having

a picnic in the park.

 read a . "Hmmm."

 and played with a .

Whoosh.

A buzzed. *BZZZZZZZ.*

The chirped. *Chirp-chirp.*

 and ate and

. *Mmmmmm.*

"My says there is a

in this park," said . "The

of a watches over the ."

"?!" screamed .

"?!" barked .

"?!" shouted and .

"BZZZZZZ, BZZZZZZ," said the

 in the 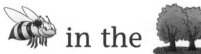.

and did not want to think about a or a . lay down to look for shapes in the .

"Like, I see a  and a ," he said. "I wonder if there's honey in that ."

"*Mmmm*," said . was hungry.

"*BZZZZZZ, BZZZZZZZ*," said the in the .

"Hey, gang, there is a 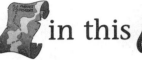 in this 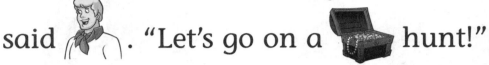,"

said . "Let's go on a  hunt!"

"We need to sniff out the ,"

said .

", where are you?" asked .

"We need some help from you now,"

said .

"Like, maybe the  of the got

!" said 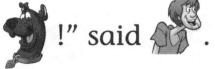.

"We have to help ," said .

8

BZZZZZZ. BZZZZZZ.

The buzzing 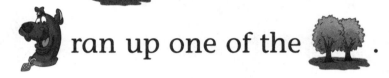 chased past

some 🌳 .

🐕 ran up one of the 🌳 .

He found some baby 🐦 in

a 🪹 .

And the 🐝 found 🐕 .

🐕 could not get away from

the 🐝 .

" , where are you?" shouted.

 and looked for near

the  .

They found slime on the  .

They found some .

The were scared.

"The of the  was

here!" said .

BZZZZZZ. BZZZZZZ.

The buzzing chased past

some kids flying .

Chirp-chirp. The were mad.

The pecked at .

 ran around the .

But the buzzing and the

 were hot on his trail.

" , where are you?" called.

 and looked for near

some kids with .

"I have some for you," said .

"Look!" said . "There is slime on

the ."

"The of the was here,"

said .

"The has !" said .

BZZZZZZ. BZZZZZZ.

The buzzing  chased Scooby to a

lake with a  .

 used the  to row extra-fast

in the .

But the  buzzed in his ear.

The covered his eyes.

The pecked at his .

 crashed the into the .

" , where are you?" called.

 saw slime on a .

 saw a buzzing .

 looked at the in her .

"I think the is near here,"

said .

"Yikes!" said . "Is the

near here, too?"

"Look, gang! found the !"

said . "There is no ."

The  buzzed. *BZZZZZZ.*

BZZZZZZ.

The chirped. *Chirp-chirp.*

 and ate with honey.

"Scooby-Dooby-Doo!"

Did you spot all the picture clues in this Scooby-Doo mystery?

Each picture clue is on a flash card. Ask a grown-up to cut out the flash cards. Then try reading the words on the back of the cards. The pictures will be your clue.

Reading is fun with Scooby-Doo!

Scooby-Doo	Fred
Velma	Daphne
Shaggy	Scooby Snacks

bee	treasure
pirate	birds
trees	ghost

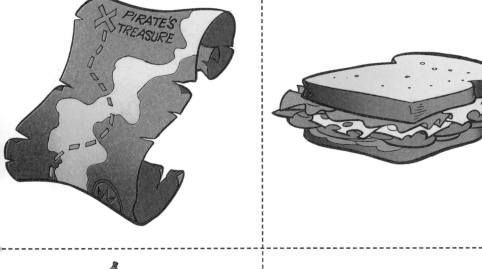

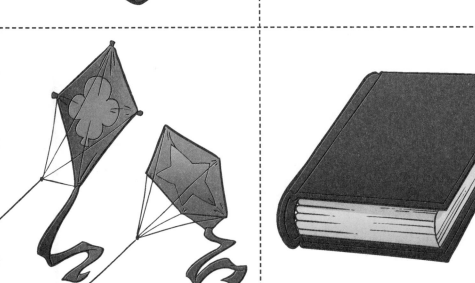

clouds	corn
sandwich	map
book	kites

boat

hive

tail

Frisbee

oars

nest